For Harry and Andrew
C.H.

For Bruce and Robert
J.H.

First published in 1991
Text copyright © J.M. Dent & Sons Ltd, 1991
Illustrations copyright © Claire Henley, 1991

Text by Fiona Kennedy and Jane Heslop.

Printed in Italy
for J.M. Dent & Sons Ltd
91 Clapham High Street
London SW4 7TA

British Library Cataloguing-in-Publication Data is available on request

The illustrations for this book were prepared using gouache paints.

FARM
DAY

Claire Henley

Dent Children's Books
London

"Cock-a-doodle-doo!"
"Time to get up," crows the cock.

Ginger, the cat,
stretches in the sun.

The pigs grunt noisily
and eat their breakfast.

The ducks splish splash
through the puddles
on their way to the pond.

The farmer drives
his big red tractor
out of the farmyard.

He's taking hay
to the sheep and lambs.

The horses gallop
in the field.

The goats jump into the garden
and eat up all the flowers.

The donkey looks over
his stable door.

Timmy, the dog, sits on the step
and chews his bone.

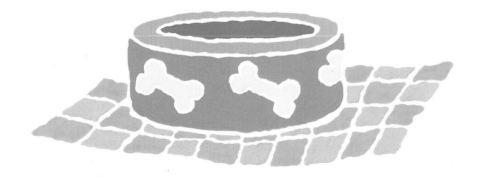

It's milking time
and the cows walk
into the milking shed.

It's getting dark.
Goodnight everyone.
See you in the morning.